It's not my fault!

It's not my fault!

BEL MOONEY

illustrated by
Margaret Chamberlain

mammoth

First published in Great Britain 1999
by Mammoth, an imprint of
Egmont Children's Books Limited
a division of Egmont Holding Limited
239 Kensington High Street, London W8 6SA

This edition first published in 2001
for The Book People Ltd
Hall Wood Avenue, Haydock, St Helens WA11 9UL

Text copyright © 1999 Bel Mooney
Illustrations copyright © 1999 Margaret Chamberlain

The moral rights of the author and illustrator have been asserted

ISBN 0 7497 2972 4

1 3 5 7 9 10 8 6 4 2

A CIP catalogue record for this title
is available from the British Library

Printed in Great Britain
by Cox & Wyman Ltd, Reading, Berkshire

Contents

A letter from Kitty

Dear Everyone

This is the eleventh book of stories about me, and I hope you like it. Lots of you already know about my friend William who lives next door, and about Rosie and Anita in my class at school. We get on well most of the time, but sometimes we have little quarrels, just like you do! Those of you who haven't read all the other stories might like to know that they start with *I Don't Want To!* which is about me when I was much younger and naughtier. I'm not at all now!

Do you ever think it's strange that people in

families aren't one bit like each other? My cousin Melissa isn't like me, but in this book you'll find out that something happens to her — which proves that we can all change. Melissa and I get on much better now.

Do you remember that at the end of *Why Me?* my mum told me she was expecting another baby, and I was jealous, although my brother Daniel was pleased? In the book called *I'm Bored!* she had the baby, and we called him Tom. You can read more about Baby Tom in this book. He's a bit of a nuisance, but we all love him a lot — except when he has a dirty nappy!

You can read these stories and see if you agree with some of the things I say and do. And if you don't . . . It's not my fault!

Lots of smiles

from

Kitty

It's not my fault!

. . . the clock goes too fast

Mornings were bad in Kitty's home. Dad rushed about telling Kitty to hurry up in the bathroom and Daniel called down that he couldn't find his games shorts, and where had Mum put them? Mum tried to shovel baby food into Tom's mouth with one hand while pushing Kitty's bread in the toaster with the other. And all the time the hands of the clock on the kitchen wall raced round as if someone had shouted 'Ready . . . steady . . . go!'

It wasn't a jolly time of day.

On this particular morning it was worse than ever. The noise was so bad that Baby Tom finally decided he would quieten them

all by making much more din himself. Kitty
looked at the angry red circle of his mouth
and wondered if there was a giant dummy
you could buy as a plug.

'Daniel – if you don't get a move on I'll be
late for work!' shouted Dad, over the cries.

At last Dad and Dan rushed out. Kitty
watched them from the step while she
waited for Mum. *Clunk* went the car doors.
Brrmmm roared the engine, as Dad put it
into reverse. Then . . . *scrrrrape*! The side of

the car made a sickening sound as it slid along the gatepost.

'Oh dear!' said Kitty.

Dad and Dan got out to look at the damage.

What Dad shouted wasn't very nice at all. To put it politely, he said the accident was all Daniel's fault for making him rush.

'It's not my fault you're a bad driver,' muttered Daniel.

'WHAT did you say?' roared Dad, his face as red as a tomato.

'Nothing!' said Dan very quickly.

They set off again and Kitty went back into the house. These days William's mother walked him and Kitty to school on her way to work, but William was off with a cold. So Kitty waited while Mum fussed over Tom – wiping his mouth, brushing the few bits of fluff she called his hair, then zipping him into his padded suit. It all seemed to take for ever.

She looked for his woolly hat, then got the pushchair out . . . She was so much *slower* since she'd had Tom.

'Oh, hurry up, Mum!' Kitty whined.

'You jolly well make sure you've got all you need for school!' snapped Mum, trying to put Tom's mittens on, while he waved his little fat hands about like windmills.

At last they were on their way. Mum kept glancing at her watch, and walked faster and faster, so that the wheels of the pushchair

whirled round and Kitty had to run to keep up. When they came near school Kitty realised there were no children walking along the street.

'Oh, Mum – we're *really* late!' she moaned.

It was true. At the school gate Mum kissed her and gave a little push, saying, 'Hurry up now, dear!'

That's all very well, thought Kitty as she ran across the empty yard, but if Mum hadn't been fussing over *that baby*, I wouldn't have to hurry at all.

All the other children were in their seats when she ran into the classroom – to find Mrs Watson glaring at her.

'Do you know what the time is, Kitty?' she asked.

'No – 'cos I haven't got a watch,' said Kitty sweetly.

'Don't be so cheeky!'

'But it's true!'

'Well, if you had a watch, maybe you wouldn't be so late,' said the teacher crossly.

'It was Baby Tom's fault I was late,' Kitty muttered.

The children laughed, and even Mrs Watson smiled – just a bit. 'Well, Kitty – even for you that's a good one. Blaming a little baby for making you late!'

It got worse. Kitty opened her schoolbag to discover she had forgotten her storybook. For homework they'd had to make up an ending for the story Mrs Watson had started reading them, and draw a picture too. Kitty liked doing that, and had taken a long time.

'Well, Kitty?' said the teacher.

'I only forgot it because Mum was making me rush,' wailed Kitty, feeling as if she wanted to cry.

'Are you sure it wasn't the baby's fault?' Mrs Watson asked – with that funny smile Kitty didn't like at all.

'It was Mum *and* the baby's fault,' said Kitty in her sulkiest voice.

As the lesson went on, she found herself thinking, in an odd part of her mind, that it was William's fault as well. If he hadn't been such a wimp to stay off school with a little cold, then his mum would have collected her on time, and then all this wouldn't have happened.

Another little voice in her mind reminded her that there'd been plenty of time to remember her own storybook, and that Mum had even reminded her to check she had everything she needed . . . But she told it to go away and be quiet.

All day Kitty felt out of sorts — as if she were a cat and someone had stroked her fur the wrong way. She made a list of all the things that were wrong.

1. Baby Tom cried too much — most of the time.

2. Daniel took ages to find his things and made Dad bad tempered.

3. The silly gate was too narrow for the car.

4. Mum fussed so over the baby — you'd think she'd never had one before.

5. William always let her down.

6. Mrs Watson made everything worse by not listening.

7. All the other children — even her best friends Rosie and Anita — wore those goody-goody faces when she got into trouble.

It simply wasn't fair. It made her feel miserable. And what's more – Kitty knew that none of it was her fault.

Mum was outside the school gates at the end of the long afternoon, and both she and Tom had big grins on their faces.

'What's the good news?' asked Kitty – without a smile.

'Nothing! We just went to the park, and had a nice time, and Tom saw some ducks and I'm sure

he tried to make a quacky sound – didn't you, my little pet?' cooed Mum.

'Gagga – gagga – gag!' said Tom.

'There you are!' cried Mum, with a smile so wide it seemed her face might split.

'Don't be silly, Mum. That's his usual stupid baby talk, that's all,' said Kitty coldly.

'Listen to this – Tom, say *quack, quack, quack*.'

'Bab – bab – baa – babba,' said Tom.

Kitty laughed scornfully. Mum looked hurt as well as irritated, and jerked the pushchair as they turned to walk home. Baby Tom didn't like that at all, and his smile disappeared.

After walking in silence for a while, Kitty asked, 'Well – did Dad ring you up and tell you about the car, then?'

'What about the car?'

'He scraped it along the gatepost this morning when he was backing out. Of course, he said it was all Dan's fault for making him rush – even though Dan wasn't driving. Great big scratch on the side. Bit surprising he didn't tell you!'

Mum stopped in her tracks. 'Oh no! That means another great big garage bill – and we simply can't afford it. Bang goes that new cooker we were saving for. Ohhhh – just wait 'til I see him . . .'

Kitty started to feel bad in a different way. She wished she hadn't mentioned the car – especially when Dad drove home from work and there was no sign of the scratch.

'Where is it?' Mum demanded.

'Where's what?' asked Dad.

'The damage to the side of the car, of course.'

'Dan – I thought we'd made a pact,' said Dad.

'I didn't say anything!' Dan protested.

'Kitty!' they both said.

'Of course she told me!' shouted Mum.

'And I think it's really sneaky of you to go and get it fixed behind my back and think you could get away with it.'

She flounced into the sitting-room and slammed the door. Kitty wished she could shrink to the size of a flea and disappear in Sandy the hamster's fur.

Dad sighed. 'If you must know, Kitty, I didn't want your mum to get upset. She gets so tired with Tom waking up so early and everything. I took it along to old Pete in the bodyshop and he did it for me quickly as a favour. Special cheap rate too.'

'Now Mum's cross, Kitty – and it's all your fault!' said Dan.

'No it's NOT!' shouted Kitty.

14

She ran up to her bedroom, slamming the door. After a few minutes she heard the sound of voices talking quietly in the sitting-room below. Then she took Mr Tubs to look out of the window, and saw Dan carrying Tom round the back garden, pointing up at the trees. The house felt peaceful suddenly, as if all the shouting of the day had never happened.

At last she went downstairs, to find Mum and Dad in the kitchen, chopping vegetables.

'Both of you . . .' Kitty began, in a small voice.

'It's all right, love, it wasn't your fault I scraped the car,' smiled Dad.

'And it was my fault you were late for school, and got cross,' said Mum, giving her a hug.

'I did make Dad get in a state,' said Dan, coming in through the kitchen door with the baby, who was gurgling happily.

'I know whose fault it all is!' cried Kitty.

'Whose?' they all asked together.

Kitty glared up at the wall and wagged her finger. 'It's that silly old clock, for going too fast!'

It's not my fault!

. . . that I'm getting older

One Saturday morning Dad woke up in such a good mood you would think he had won the lottery.

He sang in the bathroom – in his silliest, squeakiest voice. He jogged into the kitchen, gave Mum a massive hug and called her his gorgeous girlfriend – even though her eyes were puffy and her hair stuck up all over the place. It made her giggle – which made Tom chortle too.

'What's wrong with you, Dad?' asked Kitty.

'It's such a bee-oo-tiful day out there – and so I'm going to cook breakfast for everyone!' he grinned.

17

'What a good idea!' said Mum.

'Great!' said Daniel.

'Gooooo!' said Baby Tom.

'I'm not sure I feel like it,' said Kitty.

'Spoilsport!' said Dad, sticking his lips out in a silly expression, like a little boy.

Soon the sound and smell of sizzling filled the house, and secretly Kitty was sorry she had said no. It just happened sometimes. The word 'no' slipped out before she could stop it, and then she had to put up with what happened next. Sometimes she thought how good it would be if words danced about in front of your eyes for a few minutes before anyone could hear them. Then you'd have the chance to grab them and put them back where they came from if you changed your mind.

She took a piece of toast, wandered into the sitting-room and put the television on. It helped her ignore the smell of bacon and the sound of laughter that came from the kitchen. That was another thing Kitty was starting to realise – that when you said no, it sometimes made you feel lonely.

After a while she decided to telephone Rosie to see what she was planning to do that day. Rosie was still in bed, but her big sister Sara told Kitty that a couple of girls who lived in their street were coming round later to watch television. Sara was going to play them her new CD and let them try some of her make-up, and maybe even her clothes.

'Why don't you come over?' Sara suggested. 'Rosie would love that.'

Kitty was thrilled and said yes right away. She felt sure that either Mum or Dad would be glad to take her over to Rosie's house. She returned to the television programme feeling very cheerful and looking forward to the rest of the day.

Not long afterwards, Dad strode into the room, followed by Mum and Baby Tom.

'Hey, Kit-Kat – I've got a great idea for today!' he said.

'Dad wants to take you out for a treat – because Dan's off to play football, and I've decided to go to Auntie Sue's with Tom, for coffee and a chat,' Mum explained.

'What treat?' mumbled Kitty, hardly taking her eyes from the screen, where a band she liked was playing its latest hit song.

Dad picked up the remote control and zapped the television off. 'Come on, old

Square Eyes, you and I are going out on a
magical mystery tour.'

'What? . . . Where?'

'I've decided we'll go down memory lane.
You remember when you were little – what
your favourite place was?'

Kitty shook her head.

But she did remember. A few special times
Dad had taken her to Parlock Park, not far
away, just outside the next town. It was a

special place dedicated to children, with a small playground, a cafe and a museum of toys and childhood. There were old toys you could make work by pressing buttons, dolls as well as dolls' houses, a collection of ancient teddy bears which she used to think Mr Tubs liked to see . . . and so on. When she was little she thought it the best place in the world – and the fact that she and Dad were on their own made it better.

'It was Parlock Park – silly!' said Mum.

'You can bring Mr Tubs!' smiled Dad – as if he was reading Kitty's mind.

'Oh, *Dad*!' sighed Kitty.

'What?'

'Well, I'd hardly cart my *teddy* around now, would I?'

'Well, there's no law about that,' Dad said cheerfully. 'Anyway, go and get ready. We'll drop Mum at Sue's and go on from there. You can even go on the carousel! In fact –

we'll get gi–normous ice–creams and *both* ride the horses!'

'As if!' sniffed Kitty.

'Why not?'

'It's babyish!'

'Who cares?' asked Dad.

'People would think you're daft,' said Kitty, shaking her head.

'What people?'

'Any people.'

'So what?' shrugged Dad.

'In any case, I can't come with you,' Kitty said firmly, folding her arms.

'Why not?'

Kitty didn't look up. She didn't want to see Dad's face. She just muttered, 'I phoned Rosie when you were all having your breakfast and she's invited me over there.'

'Oh,' said Dad.

'What for?' asked Mum, in a voice Kitty knew well. It said, 'I-don't-think-you're-being-very-nice-and-in-a-minute-I'm-going-to-get-cross.'

'We're going to watch television, then play CDs, and Sara said we can try on her make-up and stuff like that,' Kitty said.

'Is that ALL?' snorted Mum.

'It'll be *fun*!' shouted Kitty.

'I thought you'd be pleased with my idea,' said Dad, in a voice so small it nearly got lost in his throat.

Just then Baby Tom made a very funny noise, and Mum sniffed the air. 'Oh dear,' she said.

'Pooh!' said Kitty, with an attempt at a smile.

But Mum didn't smile back. She just looked at Dad and said, 'Well, I hope you can sort something out. I'll go up and change Tom's nappy – then I'll be ready, love.'

When they were alone Dad sat down in the armchair and patted his knee. 'Come and sit here, Katfish,' he said quietly.

Kitty walked across the room and sat on the sofa just across from him. 'Oh – so you're too big and grown up to sit on my knee, is that it?' he asked.

Kitty nodded.

'Look outside,' Dad said.

Kitty turned to stare out of the window. The morning sun made the whole world look golden. Birds sang as if they'd just learned the tune and wanted to practise. Somewhere in the street, children were playing a game and laughing. Tiny fluffy white clouds chased each other across the blue sky.

'Now, do you really want to sit inside Rosie's house in front of the television with a pile of girls, putting make-up on – when we can go out into such a lovely day?' Dad asked.

Kitty didn't know what to say. She *wanted* to say 'no' this time but, instead, the word that came out was, 'yes'.

Dad gave a little sigh, then tried a laugh. 'Now, Kit, I'll make a bargain with you. I'll say that's fine, you can go to Rosie's, if you'll come over here and sit on my knee for exactly five minutes, like you used to, OK?'

Without saying anything, Kitty got up and did as he asked. Of course, she knew that as soon as she nestled on Dad's knee she wouldn't want to get up again. And the idea of the day out with him seemed nicer than ever.

'Dad?' she said.

'Yes, Kit?'

'It's not my fault, you know.'

'What isn't?'

'It's not my fault . . . that I'm getting older.'

Dad ruffled up her hair and smiled. 'I know that,' he said. 'But, on the other hand, it's not my fault that I still feel like a kid sometimes, is it?'

Kitty shook her head.

'So what shall we do?' he asked.

'Maybe we should swap jobs,' said Kitty slowly. 'I mean, you be the kid and I'll be the grown up.'

'Well, then, you have to look after me today,' said Dad with a grin.

Kitty sighed. 'Oh all right — as long as you're a good boy . . . So, what do you want to do to keep you out of mischief?'

Dad pretended to jump up and down, making Kitty bounce too. 'I know! I know! I want to go to Parlock Park. Can we do that — pleeese?'

Kitty *thought* the word 'yes!'

But she smiled, and said, 'We'll see' — just like a grown up.

It's not my fault!

. . . it got broken

Mum said that Kitty and Daniel had to look after Baby Tom while she popped next door. 'William's mum is so good at knitting, and I've really messed up this little jumper I was making for Tom,' she said. 'I need her to put me right.'

'Oh, Mum, William was coming to play with me,' moaned Kitty.

'All the better,' said Mum. 'That makes three of you to watch Tom. I want you all to stay in the sitting-room and play together. Dad's in bed with his cold, so I don't want you to make too much noise, either.'

'That's boring,' muttered Dan.

'The most boring thing in the world is children saying things are boring!' retorted Mum.

William arrived, his usual smile on his face. Kitty realised he was her happiest friend. Nothing seemed to put him in a bad mood. When she said they all had to look after the baby he said, 'That's OK.'

'No, it's not. I wanted to make a den at the bottom of the garden,' said Kitty.

'But it's raining!' said William.

'I suppose we could make one in the sitting-room – while we're looking after Tom,' said Kitty slowly.

Mum called that she wouldn't be long, and Daniel came into the sitting-room carrying the baby. When Kitty told her brother that they had decided to make a den, he grinned. Daniel always liked playing games he pretended were much too young for him, just like Kitty liked to re-read her first storybooks, with the very big print. 'Oh, all right,' sighed Dan. 'I suppose I'll have to help you.'

He put Tom's little bouncy chair on the rug and fastened the baby in it. Tom waved his arms about and shouted excitedly, as if he knew something good was about to happen.

'I know what we could do,' said William. 'Make a little house for Tom by pulling out the sofa, and putting a tablecloth or something over, and . . .'

'No – chairs would be better,' said Daniel. 'You know, like we used to do, Kit?'

'Or we could put the kitchen chairs each

31

end of the sofa to hold the tablecloth . . .' said Kitty thoughtfully.

'Then how are we going to get him in there?' asked William.

They looked round, and talked some more, and started to pull the sofa out . . . and Baby Tom started to feel bored. Nobody was looking at him, or waggling their fingers in his face and saying funny things – which is what he liked best. As far as he was concerned, nothing was happening. So he started to wave his arms about like windmills

and kick his legs — all of which made him hotter and hotter, and more and more uncomfortable . . . And that made him start to whimper.

'Oh no,' said Kitty.

'What's the matter with him?' asked William.

'Maybe he's got a pooey nappy, in which case you'll have to change it, Kit!' grinned Daniel.

'Why me?'

''Cos you're a girl — and it's a girl's job!' shouted Dan.

'What a lot of old-fashioned rubbish!' shouted Kitty. 'In any case, Dad changes nappies — so there!' She threw a cushion at her brother, but he ducked and it went rolling over the rug and just touched Tom's legs. It was gentle — but the baby didn't like it one bit.

'Waaaaaaa!'

'Now look what you've done, Kitty!' yelled Daniel.

'It wasn't my fault, it was yours — for ducking,' Kitty shouted back.

Hearing all this noise, Tom doubled his cries so that William put his hands over his ears. 'Hey, calm down, you two,' he pleaded. 'We've got to stop him crying, otherwise both our mums will hear and then we'll all get into trouble.'

'Oh — and Dad's trying to rest,' gasped Kitty, putting her hand over her mouth.

'I know — let's take him out of his chair,' said Dan sulkily. 'He likes kicking about on the floor.'

So Daniel unstrapped the baby and held him for a few minutes. Kitty got one of his toys and jangled the big bunch of plastic keys in front of his nose, until he tried to grab it and started to laugh.

'Phew!' said Dan. 'Now I'll let him lie on

the rug holding his toy, and everything'll be all right.'

He put the baby down and the room was filled with the sound of his contented gurglings. Kitty and William went back to trying to work out how the den should be, and Dan said he would go into the kitchen for some biscuits and juice. Then Kitty followed Daniel out, to bring back a chair, and William took all the cushions off the sofa to stack behind it, making a little house.

Minutes passed. Kitty came back and disappeared behind the furniture. William started to tickle her and she got the giggles. Daniel was still in the kitchen trying to get the lid off the biscuit tin . . .

None of them could have dreamed what Baby Tom would do next. He had thrown his toy to one side and wanted to get it. A hidden camera would have seen the baby kick and

kick, and lean more and more to one side. At
last he rolled himself on his tummy – where
he wanted to be. For a short time he lay there
like a little frog, 'swimming' in the air. Then
he pushed himself up on his arms, which he
did all the time. But something made him
pull up one leg, then the other . . .

At last Daniel came back into the room,
carrying a plate of biscuits. Still William and
Kitty were behind the sofa, trying to get a
cloth to drape over the kitchen chair . . .

'I'll just go back for the juice,' called Daniel.
'Have a bisc–'

He stopped.

'Oh no! Where have you put the baby?'

Kitty and William poked their heads up
over the back of the sofa, and both looked
amazed.

'He's on the r–' Kitty began. Then stared.

There was no baby on the rug, where she had last seen him. Frantically the three children looked around the room. And there in the far corner they saw him, moving along the carpet. But Tom couldn't crawl. The surprise made them all gawp at him with open mouths, like three goldfish in a bowl. And all the time Tom was struggling towards a table in the corner, covered with a lovely trailing cloth . . .

'Watch out!' Kitty shouted.

Dan dropped the plate of biscuits and ran across the room, tripping over a stool on the way.

'Goo-goo,' laughed Tom happily, loving his new freedom. He arrived at the table and seized the cloth in his little fat fist – and tugged. One of Mum's favourite china ornaments – a pretty lady in a Victorian dress – started to wobble and sway . . .

'It might fall on his head!' shouted William.

'Quickly!' Kitty shrieked at Dan.

Daniel made a dive, just in time to catch hold of the ornament that tumbled – *plop*! – into his outstretched hands. William and Kitty started to clap – but it was too soon.

The cloth fell on top of Tom, who started to yell again. Daniel was so worried about the baby he didn't look where he was putting his feet, and fell over the other end of the cloth. The ornament flew into the air and – *crash*! – on to the floor.

By the time William and Kitty had run forward, Daniel had uncovered Tom's head.

He was so pleased to see his brother he started to shout with joy.

Just then the door flew open – and there were the two mums, and Dad in his pyjamas with his red nose.

'Wass all the doise?' sniffed Dad.

'What have you done!' cried Mum, looking at the Victorian lady who lay in pieces on the floor. 'WHO broke that?'

'It wasn't my fault, Mum,' said Dan, pathetically.

'Did you drop it?' demanded Mum.

'Yes, but . . .'

'Well, I thought I could trust you, Dan. Look at all this mess. You're really naughty!' shouted Mum, almost in tears.

'That's not fair, Mum,' said Kitty.

'It was Tom who broke it – really,' said William.

'I think you should keep out of it, Bill,' said William's Mum, with a warning look.

'But, Mum, you've got to listen,' said Kitty. 'Tom *did* break it because he pulled the cloth off the table, and Daniel saved it, but then he had to save Tom and . . .'

Kitty's mum turned to William and demanded that he tell her exactly what had happened. He told the whole story, as simply as he could, and was rewarded by delight on all the adults' faces.

'Are you saying . . .?' began Dad.

'Oh, that's so thrilling,' said William's mum.

'My clever Tom,' cooed Mum, rushing across the room and scooping up Tom in her arms. 'Who's a big boy, then?'

Oh yuk, thought

Kitty. Why is it that a baby gets *praised* for breaking something? Grown-ups are pretty nutty really . . .

William just smiled and smiled.

'There you are!' said Dan, folding his arms. 'I told you it wasn't my fault!'

'I tell you what, though,' said Kitty. 'I think we all deserve a reward for teaching Tom to crawl! That *was* our fault!'

It's not my fault!

. . . that they quarrelled

Kitty had a habit she found hard to break. If somebody told her a secret, she just could not keep it to herself. It was as if her tongue was like a little red bird who would fly out of the cage without warning, and chirrup the news.

Mum said she wouldn't tell Kitty what she had bought Dad or Dan for Christmas or birthdays because it might slip out. It wasn't that Kitty meant to tell. She'd smile and whisper, 'I know something you don't know', start to drop little hints, then big ones . . . And before too long there was a good guess, and the secret was out. She didn't *mean* any harm. It was just all too exciting.

The trouble is – there are family secrets and there are private things people say, and it doesn't always do to speak when you could stay quiet.

As they walked to school with his mum, William was telling Kitty what he liked and didn't like about different people in their class. There was a new boy called Jason Edwards, who was already very popular. William really wanted to be his friend – but Jason was one of those boys everybody likes because he is good at everything and very confident.

'I don't think he's even noticed me,' said William.

'Never mind, William, you can always hang round with us,' said Kitty kindly. Which wasn't really what William wanted to hear.

'I don't always want to be with girls,' he said. 'And in any case, Rosie gets on my nerves. When she laughs she sounds like a hyena.'

This made Kitty giggle, and William joined in. He did a few imitations of Rosie's laugh, until Kitty was helpless – and his mum told them not to be silly.

Kitty forgot all about this when she met Rosie in the cloakroom. They talked about the school fair, and Kitty asked Rosie which stall she was going to volunteer for.

'I thought the "throw-the-sponge",' said Rosie. 'If we can persuade one of the teachers to sit there as the target! Do you want to do it with me?'

'I thought you'd promised Anita to run a stall with her,' said Kitty, pleased.

'To be honest, Kit, Anita's too shy. You have to shout out and get people to come along and have a go. It's no good just sitting there like a mouse.'

'I suppose not,' said Kitty. 'Well, I'll help you, if you like.'

At break Kitty stayed behind to ask Mrs Watson something, so she was leaving the classroom just as Jason Edwards came back in to get something he'd forgotten.

'Hallo. How d'you like our school, then?' she asked.

'It's OK,' said Jason.

'Listen, you should talk to William. He's really nice – and he'd like to be your friend,' Kitty blurted.

There were a couple of boys standing behind Jason – two of the biggest and toughest in the class – and they started to

snigger. 'Oooh, little Billy wants to be Jason's fwend,' said one of them in a squeaky voice.

Jason was a friendly boy, and secretly felt rather overwhelmed by the new school. But he hid it by seeming to be very 'cool'. So he just gave a little grin, shrugged and went past Kitty into the classroom.

Now Kitty went looking for Anita – to tell her that she was going to do the stall with Rosie, so that Anita would have plenty of time to think of something else. 'But why can't all three of us run a stall together?' her friend asked.

'Oh, Rosie wants to do that funny wet sponge one and she says you have to shout about it and it's no good standing there quietly like a mouse.'

'So she says I'm like a mouse?' Anita asked, looking cross as well as hurt. Kitty nodded. Then, trying to make Anita smile, she added, 'That's OK – William says Rosie laughs like a hyena!'

'Huh,' said Anita, tossing her plait back over her shoulder.

The bell went and there was no more time for talking. They all trooped back into the classroom and soon Mrs Watson was telling them all about how volcanos happen and Kitty was so interested she didn't think about anything else.

But when it came to the middle of the day there was an eruption Kitty hadn't expected.

Anita marched up to Rosie and said she didn't think it was fair that she'd gone behind her back and decided Kitty should be on the stall, but that anyway *she* didn't want to be with someone with an embarrassing laugh like a hyena.

'Who says that?' Rosie demanded, folding her arms.

'William!' shrieked Anita.

William was standing nearby. When Rosie asked if he'd said that about her, he nodded nervously. Rosie glared at Anita and William. 'Well, I'd rather be a big tough hyena than a stupid little mouse. And you're a mouse too, William – otherwise you'd stand up for yourself when the boys laugh at you!'

'Who's laughing?' William asked.

'Jason and all them – 'cos they're all saying you want to be Jason's friend and he doesn't want to be friends with a wimp,' snapped Rosie.

The other children, who were listening to the quarrel, started to laugh – especially the boys.

William went very red, and shouted that he wasn't a wimp and that Rosie should mind her own business.

'Well, don't you go round calling people names,' said Rosie.

'You called *me* a name, Rosie,' said Anita. 'I suppose you think it's all right for YOU!'

It was horrible. Kitty watched from a distance then crept away. But she wasn't quick enough. William spotted her and came running after her, taking her arm.

'Why did you tell somebody what I said about Jason?' he hissed.

Then Rosie and Anita followed and the three of them all stared at her with tight, angry faces.

'This is all your fault, Kitty,' said Anita.

'It's nothing to do with me — it's *your* silly childish quarrel!' said Kitty, putting on her loftiest expression.

But she knew that wasn't true. The others all went away, not speaking to each other or to her, and all afternoon Kitty had an uncomfortable feeling in her stomach — like she got when she had to go to the dentist.

After school, Kitty's mum was waiting

outside the school gate with Baby Tom. William told her that he wasn't going to go home with them, but would walk along the High Street to see his mother at the cake shop where she worked. He had done that before, so Kitty's mother didn't think anything was wrong.

Kitty shuffled along with her head down, not speaking. From time to time Mum would

look at her, puzzled, and try to start a conversation. Kitty stayed quiet.

'What's the matter with you this afternoon?' Mum asked at last.

'Nothing!' said Kitty – much too quickly.

But when they got inside the house she couldn't help it. She ran upstairs for Mr Tubs, brought him downstairs to cuddle – and burst into tears. Mum put Tom in his highchair with a pile of things to play with and took both Kitty and her teddy on her knee.

Kitty told her the whole story, not missing anything out. 'Oh dear,' said Mum. 'Well, it's all a bit complicated, but it sounds as if everybody was pretty nasty.'

'Yes,' sniffed Kitty. 'And they all think it's my fault.'

'Well . . . whose fault do *you* think it is?' Mum asked slowly.

There was a long silence. Kitty chewed Mr

Tubs's ear while she thought and thought. At last she mumbled, 'Mine.'

Mum nodded. She let Kitty think for a while, then whispered, 'Well, you've taken the first important step to putting it right.'

'What's that?'

'Owning up to yourself. Now the bravest thing comes next.'

'I suppose that's owning up to them?'

Mum shook her head. 'No – they already know who did the tittle-tattling. What you have to do now is be very brave, and say sorry.'

And Kitty said, 'I know.'

It's not my fault!

. . . that she's a pain

It was terrible news. It was the worst news Kitty had heard that year. It made Daniel laugh and laugh, until she chased him round the room.

Uncle Joe and Auntie Susan were moving house to live this side of town. But that wasn't the worst thing. It meant that Melissa would go to Kitty's school!

'You'll have to look after her, love,' said Mum.

'No chance!' said Kitty.

'What did you say?' demanded Mum.

'I said I don't want to,' replied Kitty, folding her arms and staring back at her mother with a furious expression.

'Why not?' asked Dad.

Kitty thought, as she did so often nowadays, that the G-Us were impossible. Grown-ups think that you have to like their friends' children. Worse, they believe that everybody in a family has to be friendly, simply because they're related. And it doesn't work like that – as Kitty knew well.

'Because nobody will like her — and I didn't choose to have her as a cousin!' shouted Kitty.

'But you'll take her round a bit?' pleaded Mum.

'Pretend you're a sheepdog, and she's a sheep!' sniggered Dan.

'That's enough, Daniel,' said Dad.

'Anyway, I shall be very disappointed if you don't look after your cousin,' said Mum in a firm voice.

A month passed, and Mum spent a lot of time at Auntie Susan's house, helping her get ready for the move.

'They'll need a whole separate van for all Melissa's clothes and stuff!' Kitty said to Dan, who grinned.

At last the removal van did its work, and the following Monday Melissa was to start at Kitty's school. Kitty's mum arranged to meet Auntie Susan and Melissa at the gates, so that the girls could go in together. Kitty dreaded it.

When she saw Melissa she felt even worse. Her cousin was dressed up as if she was going to a party – although no one Kitty knew would choose to wear clothes like that to go *anywhere*.

'Hallo, Kitty,' said Melissa nervously.

'Hi,' said Kitty, looking over Melissa's shoulder.

'You *will* look after her, love, won't you?' smiled Auntie Susan, as she bent to give Melissa a goodbye kiss.

'Of course she will,' said Mum, giving Kitty a warning look.

So the girls went into school together – or, at least, nearly together, because Kitty walked a couple of paces in front of Melissa, pretending she was in a hurry. 'Wait for me, Kitty!' puffed Melissa.

All the children stared as Kitty led her cousin into their classroom. Kitty wanted the earth to open up and swallow her, and she

saw one or two of the children point to Melissa's shiny shoes, and grin.

'Ah, this is our new girl – Kitty's cousin, Melissa,' said Mrs Watson, patting Melissa on the head. 'Now, everybody, I want you all to make Melissa really welcome. And, of course, Kitty will take charge of her this first week, to make sure she meets everybody and knows where everything is.'

Kitty cringed and went to her place without looking at her cousin.

Of course, Mrs Watson put Melissa next to her – moving Anita to do so. This made Kitty angrier than ever. How dare her silly old cousin come to her school and spoil everything?

At break all the children streamed out into the yard. Melissa stuck to Kitty's side like a limpet and complained loudly when Kitty said she wanted to go and swing on the huge climbing frame with Rosie and the others. 'That's stupid!' she said.

'Come on, Kit,' said Rosie.

'Don't go – stay with me,' begged Melissa.

Rosie gave Melissa an unfriendly look, and moved off. Kitty ran after her, and said she would do her best to shake her cousin off. 'It's not my fault she's a pain, Rosie,' she whispered.

'I know,' shrugged Rosie, and gave Kitty a little friendly pat to show she understood.

By the end of the day, Kitty was thoroughly fed up with her cousin. She didn't bother to talk to anybody much, and so they didn't bother to talk to her. She put her hand up too much in class, so that it looked like she was showing off. When she opened her lunch-box she made a great point of telling Kitty in a very loud voice that her mother only gave her healthy food, and she was never ever allowed to eat chocolate, sugar or junk food . . . It all got on Kitty's nerves, even more than usual. That was because she was seeing her cousin through other people's eyes. And *they* clearly thought Melissa *was* a pain.

By the end of the day there was something else wrong with Kitty, too. She felt strange, as

if somebody had pummelled her all over. She didn't want to eat her tea, and felt generally out of sorts.

'Did you look after Melissa, Kitty?' Mum asked.

'Look, Mum – it's not my fault her mum's your sister! I don't like her, and that's that! She made my day really horrible, and it's all *her* fault I feel so rotten now.'

But it wasn't Melissa's fault at all. Next morning Kitty woke up to find Mr Tubs all damp in bed beside her. She was very hot, her head ached, and she couldn't breathe. 'MU–UM!' she yelled. 'I don't feel well!'

The sneezing started that very minute, and by the time Mum came upstairs Kitty's whole bed was shaking. With a pink face and streaming eyes she was a very sorry sight.

'Oh dear,' said Mum. 'You've caught Dad's cold. No school for you, Kitsy!'

Kitty tossed around, slept a little, made her headache worse with sneezing, and generally felt bad all morning. She listened to a story-tape, but went back to sleep in the middle of it, and woke feeling more frustrated than ever. She heard Mum singing to Baby Tom, and felt jealous. And she thought how unfair it is that you can never stay off school when you're well enough to read, draw and play, but only when you don't want to do anything at all.

While Tom was having his nap, Mum came up with some hot blackcurrant juice

and sat on Kitty's bed for a chat. That made Kitty feel better. After a while Mum said, 'I wonder how Melissa's getting on without you there to look after her.'

For some reason, the nice way Mum said that made Kitty feel a little bit guilty. So she explained to Mum in her snuffly voice that Melissa could do a lot more to make people like her.

'Well, maybe you should tell her,' said Mum.

'Why me?'

'Because it would be best coming from you. Remember that time William's friends and cousins were teasing her, and you stuck up for her?'

'Ye-es.'

'Well, you gave her a little talking to then, and for a while she listened, didn't she? Why not try again? After all, Kit – if it works it'll make life better for *you*, won't it?'

Kitty realised that was true. Unwillingly she asked Mum what she thought she should do.

'Telephone her tonight.'

'Oh no! I'm not well enough,' whined Kitty.

'Well, write her a letter! You got that lovely writing paper with dolphins on it for your birthday – and Dad's going over tonight to help Joe put up some shelves, so he can take it.'

Kitty knew now that she had no choice. Looking pleased, Mum made her pillows comfortable, and brought her a tray to lean on, as well as the writing paper.

'I'll leave you to it,' she said cheerfully – and left Kitty chewing the pen and wishing she had never agreed to this plan. She thought and thought, and couldn't make herself tell Melissa the truth. At last she looked down and saw Mr Tubs looking at her with that funny lopsided expression.

'Just get on with it, Kitty!' he seemed to be saying. And that gave her the idea.

This was the letter that went to Melissa that Tuesday evening.

Der Mellissa

Kitty arskked mi to writ to you. I sory I cannt spell and don no meni words. Kit tole mi yoo are ot her skool and wanta mek frens. This is wot yoo do.

1. Smil a lot and arsk peple about theyself

2. Don show oft – abowt ennything ATT AL

3. Wer cloths lik the othes wer and not posh cloths

4. Join in thinks evin if you don wan to.

5. Only say nice thinks – like tellink Rosie you like herstile or sumfhink.

I cannt thinkg of ennythink els but this will help you. Last – I have writ a pome for you.

DON THIINK OF YOU BUT THINK OF THEM, AN THEN THELL WANT TO BE YOUR FREN.

God luk from

MR TUBS (Kittys Teddy)

65

Kitty's cold was so bad, Mum was afraid it would turn into flu and so she kept Kitty in bed for the rest of the week. By the weekend she felt better, although still Mum wouldn't let her go out. On Monday she was dying to get back to school.

'I wonder how Melissa's got on without me,' she said to Mum.

'Well, Auntie Sue says . . .' Mum paused, then smiled and added, 'Never mind.'

Kitty's first shock came when she entered the classroom. Anita was back in her old place (and SO pleased to see her!) but where was Melissa? Kitty looked round, greeted her friends, but couldn't see her cousin anywhere. Then she noticed a girl with short curly blonde hair sitting next to Jason Edwards, with her back to Kitty, shaking with laughter at something he had said. Who was it? Surely it couldn't be . . .

It was Melissa! She turned round and

gave Kitty a cheerful wave, just as Mrs Watson came in and said good morning to them all. Kitty stared at her cousin – and couldn't stop staring. She didn't even hear Mrs Watson ask them all to get out their rough books.

Melissa looked like a completely different girl. Gone were the fussy ribbons and droopy curls she used to be so proud of.

Gone were the pale tights, shiny party-shoes, and neat little skirts and dresses. Today she wore a grey hooded sweat top over plain navy cotton trousers with pockets on the side of the legs, and navy trainers with an orange flash. And the short hair made her look . . . well, great!

Kitty felt dazed. She couldn't wait for break to come so that she could see if Melissa had changed in any other ways as well. When the bell rang they all got up with a clatter. To Kitty's amazement, Melissa didn't even wait for her, but walked out of the classroom so confidently with Jason and his friends that Kitty almost felt a twinge of envy.

Rosie came up behind her and stuck her arm in Kitty's. 'We all think your cousin's really cool, Kit,' she smiled. 'Hey, Mel — wait for us!'

Mel?

The smile Melissa gave Kitty would have lit

up a dark room at midnight. She looked so relaxed and happy that Kitty felt she was meeting her for the first time.

'Kit – did you know Jason's got a new puppy he's called Dan?' her cousin asked.

'I wonder if he's as noisy and naughty as my ol' brother,' said Kitty, with a dazed smile.

'He's invited a crowd of us over to his place next Saturday to play with it. William's coming,' said Melissa.

'You too, Kitty – if you want to,' Jason interrupted.

Kitty felt as if she was dreaming. She looked her cousin up and down, and in the end she couldn't help herself. She had to take her to one side and find out.

'You look fabulous, Melissa . . .'

'Listen, will you do me a favour and call me Mel? Everybody else does now,' said her cousin.

'OK . . . er . . . Mel. But where'd you get the clothes and everything?'

'I had some birthday money. And I got Mum to take me shopping. She was a bit hurt I didn't want to wear the clothes she chose any more, but . . .' She shrugged.

'Sometimes you have to hurt the G–Us' feelings.'

Kitty nodded. 'Listen – I hope she didn't think it was my fault.'

'Why?'

'Because . . . well, you know.'

Melissa laughed. 'But it's nothing to do with *you*, Kitty, is it? It's all the doing of that very wise teddy bear who hangs round your house!'

It's not my fault!

. . . that the stars are out of reach

One day a day came that nobody wanted to come. But such days do arrive, when the time is right, and there is nothing we can do to stop them . . .

Gran was getting very old, and now she was ill again. She was very sick indeed and Mum and Dad were terribly worried. They took turns with Auntie Susan and Uncle Joe to sit with her in hospital, and every few days Melissa, Daniel or Kitty went too – because seeing the children cheered Gran up a lot. To be honest, none of them liked going to visit because it made them so sad. But Dan said if it made Gran happy that

was far more important, and Kitty knew he was right.

The weeks passed, and Kitty tried to get on with life in her normal way – which meant quarrelling the usual small amount with Dan, Melissa, and all her friends, and telling Mr Tubs her troubles at night. Oh, and not cleaning out the hamster's cage in the hope that somebody else might do it, and then pretending she had forgotten.

But life couldn't really go on as usual, because of Gran. It was as if a dark blueygrey cloud hung over the house all the time and no breeze could blow it away. That's what Kitty thought.

She asked Mum if Gran was going to be all right, and could see from her face that it wasn't the right question. But a second later Mum put a bright smile on, like a mask, and said, 'Of course, pet!'

'How's your Gran, Kit?' asked Rosie in school.

Kitty shrugged, not trusting herself to speak.

'She will get better, won't she?' asked Anita.

'Of course she will!' said William.

But Kitty said nothing.

That night Kitty crept into Daniel's room when it was quite late and they both had their lights out. He was wide awake too.

'Can I talk to you, Danny?' she asked.

'Yes – OK, Kit,' said her brother.

'Can you hear them downstairs?'

'Yes, I've been listening.'

Through the floor they heard a soft sound of voices, and a little crying too. Mum was obviously very upset, and Dad was talking to her. Kitty and Dan sat in silence for a while, just listening – and understanding exactly what was going on, even if they couldn't hear the words.

'Dan . . . er . . . can I ask you . . .?' Kitty began.

He shook his head. 'Please don't, Kit.'

'But you have to talk about things, don't you?' she wailed. 'Otherwise how can you understand them?'

'I suppose so,' said her brother unwillingly.

'Gran isn't ever going to get better, is she?' demanded Kitty.

'Yes, she jolly well *is*!' Dan said stubbornly – so that Kitty knew there was no point in talking to him any more. Suddenly she felt much older than her big brother, so she patted him on the shoulder, said goodnight, and tiptoed to her own room.

Now Kitty felt very wide awake and didn't want to go back to bed. She pulled her curtains apart and looked out of the window. What she saw made her gasp. The whole garden, like all the other gardens that backed on to theirs, was silver and black. The moonlight was so bright she could see all the stakes of the fence, and the piles of plantpots and the wheelbarrow in the corner, and the shed, as if somebody had gone round the outlines with a Christmassy silver marker.

The moon hung in the sky like a great big glittering plate – completely round and much bigger than Kitty had ever seen it. But that wasn't the only marvellous thing on this magical night. There were so many stars! The whole sky sparkled with mysterious patterns, weaving in and out and up and down, and all over the Universe.

'Hallo, moon. Hallo, stars,' Kitty whispered, without knowing why – but thinking how generous it was that they made the whole country silvery and beautiful, even though most people didn't see.

Then she decided to make a wish – a big wish, a wish as huge as the sky outside. She remembered a song she'd heard a long time ago, about wishing on a star, and picked

the brightest one she could see, stared at it
for a long time, then shut her eyes tightly, so
that it glowed red in the dark green inside

her head, like a comforting fire. '*I wish Gran would get better,*' she said aloud. Then added, '*Please, star.*'

Kitty stood there for a long time, staring at the stars until they seemed to come closer and closer and fill her eyes, her mind and her room. Kitty knew they were her friends, and would make her wish come true. The thought made her feel better. But at last she yawned, and felt a bit chilly. So she turned back to her bed, clung to Mr Tubs, and fell happily down into the warm darkness.

Gran died later that night, peacefully in her sleep, when Kitty and Dan and Melissa and their parents were all in their beds, and the moon and the stars were fading in the sky of morning.

Then it was a sad time of telephone calls and talking and tears. Mum and Dad sat down with Kitty and Daniel and told them that Gran had been very old, and had had a lovely busy life and loved them all very much, and now she was at rest at last. Kitty knew it was true, but it didn't stop her remembering all the presents Gran had given her, and the way she looked after her when Kitty was very little, and how she always had a twinkle in her eye when she gave them those knitted clothes that were usually too big. Gran was lovely. Kitty missed her and felt terribly sad.

'Nothing will change that either, love,' said Mum – much later, when Gran's funeral was over and they all knew they had to get on with their lives, just like Gran would have wanted.

'I know,' said Kitty, sniffing a little. 'But it's not fair.'

'Oh, you always used to say that,' said Mum with a small smile.

'I made a wish, too,' said Kitty resentfully.

'When?' Mum asked.

'The night Gran died. I made a special wish on a special star, but I think it was too far away to hear. And now I hate that silly old star.'

'Oh, Kit-Kat,' said Mum. 'Don't make things worse. Don't waste your energy hating poor old stars when it's not their fault at all.'

'But I want to blame somebody!' Kitty wailed.

'Listen, love, I decided a long time ago that the stars are out of reach. It's not their fault and its not my fault – no more than it's your fault that your wish didn't come true. All it means is you can't help things happening – do you understand?'

'I suppose so,' said Kitty, cuddling up on Mum's knee.

Still Kitty couldn't stop being a rebel. That night she looked out of her window for the stars, wanting to give them a good talking to – but it was a very cloudy night and the sky was dark.

She thought how sad it was her mum had given up wishing, because it made you feel a lot happier when you thought you might be able to change things. Those stars that night had *seemed* so close . . . And Kitty always liked to believe what she wanted to believe, not necessarily what grown-ups told her. After all, how did they *know* they were right? You couldn't know!

As she looked out on the dark garden, she remembered a day when Gran came over to play with her, and they had sat outside for ages having a picnic with the plastic tea-set and Mr Tubs and the other cuddly toys. Gran was always so patient and sweet – pretending to eat and drink when there was nothing there at all. 'I can see things other people can't see, sweetheart,' she had said. 'Don't you listen to people who tell you you can't believe whatever you like!'

Kitty seemed to hear her now, saying that. And it was as if Gran herself was putting the wonderful idea into her head.

The next day, before school, Kitty counted the money in her moneybox. She pulled a face, and went to find Dad.

'Pleeeese will you give me some pocket money in advance, Dad?' she begged. 'I need to buy a special thing for Mum.' She knew he couldn't refuse – and he didn't.

As luck would have it, William's mum was meeting them from school that day, and Kitty asked if they could go to the toy shop in the High Street. She wouldn't explain why, because she knew now that some secret plans are so special you spoil them by talking about them – like lighting a candle on a bright day. But William and his mum didn't mind when she said she was planning something nice for her mum. They wandered happily round the shop, while Kitty bought several packs of what she needed – using up all her money.

She couldn't wait to get home, although

it would be hours before her plan would work.

They had all eaten, and Kitty and Daniel had done their homework and watched a little television, when Mum told Kitty to go to bed.

'I'll come up and read you a story in a minute, if you like.'

'No, it's OK, Mum,' Kitty replied. 'I'm reading my storybook from school, and I really want to finish it. You have a rest!'

'Good girl!' said Dad.

Kitty kissed them goodnight and went upstairs. She got what she needed from her room, then crept into Mum and Dad's bedroom, being very careful not to touch the cot where Baby Tom lay fast asleep. The room was full of light from the landing, so she could see what she was doing.

It took some time for Kitty to finish. There were swirls and patterns, she remembered, and she wanted it to be just perfect. At last she had finished, and she hurried back to her own room to put her pyjamas on.

The long wait began then, and it nearly drove Kitty mad. First Daniel came up to bed, and Kitty heard him messing about next door for a long time. At last his room fell quiet.

Kitty could still hear the noises from downstairs. Luckily Mum and Dad went to bed much earlier these days, because they said they were tired out after all that had happened. So Kitty kept herself awake and waited.

She knew their routine very well. She'd hear Dad go into the kitchen to check that the back door was locked, and fill the kettle ready for morning. Then they'd come upstairs, put on their bedside light, and change Tom's nappy. They'd take turns to go into the bathroom, and Mum would take ages putting on her face cream . . .

'Oh, please don't feel like a bath tonight, Mum!' whispered Kitty.

Luckily Mum didn't. The minutes passed, and Kitty crept out of bed to stand at the door of her room, which was always slightly ajar, like her parents' door. She ached for the moment when they would settle Tom and finally put out their light . . .

It was nearly time. She left her room and tiptoed across the landing as silently as possible.

Click — went the light.

Kitty waited. Then she heard one of them stir, and sit up. At the same time Tom started a delighted gurgling and gooing noise.

'Look, love!' said Dad's voice.

'Whatever . . .?' whispered Mum, in wonder.

Kitty couldn't stop herself. She peeped round their door – to see that her plan had worked even better than she had imagined. The room was full of a ghostly, silvery light, and all round the window – as if they had swirled in from the darkness outside – the glow-stars glimmered on the wall. It looked so beautiful Kitty didn't know whether she wanted to laugh or cry.

'Who . . .?' Dad began.

'Kitty, of course,' said Mum softly.

'I'm here, Mum,' called Kitty.

'Of course you are!' replied Mum, holding out her arms.

The three of them sat on the bed and looked at the wonderful wall of stars. Then Dad got up and fetched Tom, who smiled and smiled and reached out to the glowing things with both his hands.

Nobody spoke. But Daniel must have heard something, because now he appeared at the door of the room and came to sit on the bed, too.

'Did Kitty do that?' he asked.

'Who else?' asked Dad.

'Why?' asked Dan, looking at his sister.

'Well — I wanted to prove something to Mum. She said the stars are out of reach, but I've proved they aren't. You can touch these

stars, Mum – and they're all for our gran,' said Kitty proudly.

Of course, Mum couldn't say a word, but she didn't need to. Because Tom amazed them all by pointing and babbling, 'Sta – sta – sta – sta!'

'He's talking about *you*, Kits,' said Mum at last.